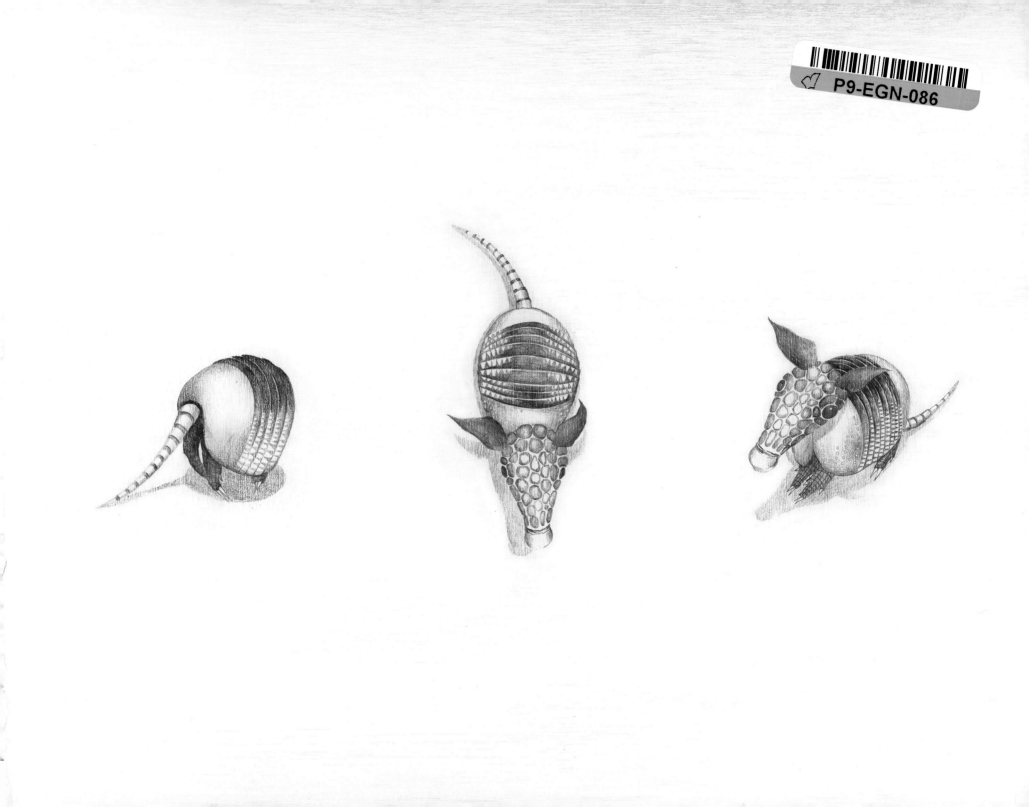

An Armadillo in NEW YORK

Julie Kraulis

Tundra Books

To my sisters and brothers: Bene and Christophe, Crick and Jonathan, Andrew and T.

Tundra Books, a division of Random House of Canada Limited, a Penguin Random House Company

Library and Archives Canada Cataloguing in Publication

Kraulis, Julie, author, illustrator
An armadillo in New York / Julie Kraulis.

Issued in print and electronic formats.
ISBN 978-1-77049-891-4 (BOUND).– ISBN 978-1-77049-893-8 (EPUB)

I. Title.

PS8621.R37A75 2016   jC813'.6   C2015-901056-X   C2015-901057-8

Published simultaneously in the United States of America by Tundra Books of Northern New York, a division of Random House of Canada Limited, a Penguin Random House Company

Library of Congress Control Number: 2015931501

Edited by Samantha Swenson
The artwork in this book was rendered in oils and graphite.
The text was set in Adobe Caslon and Justlefthand.
Printed and bound in China

Sources:
The website of the National Parks Service: http://www.nps.gov/stli/index.htm
The website of the United Nations Educational, Scientific and Cultural Organization (UNESCO): http://whc.unesco.org/en/list/307
Sutherland, Cara A. (2003). *The Statue of Liberty*. New York City: Barnes & Noble Books.

www.penguinrandomhouse.ca

1   2   3   4   5   20   19   18   17   16

TUNDRA BOOKS | Penguin Random House

Arlo feels it. The twitch in his left claw. The twitch that only stops when adventure begins …

This is Arlo, an armadillo from Brazil. He loves to explore! He inherited his love for adventure from his grandfather Augustin. In fact, curiosity has run in their nine-banded tribe for as long as anyone can remember.

When Arlo was born, Augustin wrote him a collection of travel journals about his favorite places in the world so that one day Arlo could use them on his own travels. Today Arlo is reading the journal about New York City and the famous Lady Liberty and getting ready to start off on another adventure!

Augustin & Arlo

Dearest Arlo, New York is one of the most exciting cities in the world, a place with a pulsing heartbeat. I cannot wait for you to discover the amazing architecture, interesting history and vibrant culture. You'll especially love meeting Lady Liberty. Follow the path I've laid out in my journal and you will learn all about her — and even get to meet her! Go take your bite of the Big Apple, Arlo!

ONCE YOU LAND, MAKE YOUR WAY TO THE VERY TOP OF ROCKEFELLER CENTER, ONE OF NEW YORK'S MOST BELOVED SKYSCRAPERS. YOU CAN SEE THE WHOLE CITY FROM THERE, INCLUDING CENTRAL PARK, TIMES SQUARE, THE HUDSON RIVER AND THE FAMOUS EMPIRE STATE BUILDING. LADY LIBERTY IS VERY TALL, AND SHE HAS A GREAT VIEW OF THE CITY TOO.

After a flight north across the Atlantic Ocean, Arlo catches a taxi into the heart of New York City. First stop: Top of the Rock! He's amazed — the cars and people look like ants.

IT'S HARD TO SEE THE STARS IN THE CITY WITH ALL THE BRIGHT LIGHTS AND TOWERING BUILDINGS, BUT YOU CAN SEE SOME GREAT CONSTELLATIONS AT GRAND CENTRAL TERMINAL. STARGAZING IS ONE OF LADY LIBERTY'S FAVORITE THINGS TO DO, AND SHE HAS A PERFECT SPOT FOR IT!

Arlo makes his way to Grand Central Terminal. It's the start of the day, but the ceiling of the main hall is filled with the night sky. Arlo hopes he gets to stargaze with Lady Liberty someday.

YOUR NEXT STOP IS JUST AROUND THE CORNER: THE NEW YORK PUBLIC LIBRARY. LADY LIBERTY LOVES BOOKS AND ALWAYS HAS ONE IN HAND. HERE YOU'LL MEET HER FAVORITE LIONS, PATIENCE AND FORTITUDE. THEY KEEP WATCH OVER A GRAND COLLECTION OF BOOKS.

Arlo makes friends with the lions at the library. They are quite a regal pair! Lady Liberty sure has interesting friends.

ARLO, WANDER AROUND BROADWAY TO SEE THE THEATERS THAT ARE FILLED EVERY NIGHT WITH GREAT ACTORS AND PERFORMANCES. THE MARQUEES LIGHT UP THE NIGHT FOR THEATERGOERS, JUST AS LADY LIBERTY ONCE LIT UP THE NIGHT FOR SEAFARERS.

Arlo walks through the theater district imagining what it would be like on opening night. Lady Liberty must also dazzle against the night sky.

Next up is the Guggenheim Museum. Here you will find a gallery on a spiraling ramp with an exciting collection of modern art, including many great French works. It was a French sculptor, Frédéric Bartholdi, who brought Lady Liberty to America, and she quickly became one of New York's greatest treasures.

Arlo walks around and around, higher and higher, taking in the art at the Guggenheim. Lady Liberty must be pretty special. Who could she be?

Arlo eats a pretzel, tacos and some
New York–style pizza. All this walking
has made him very hungry!

GET AWAY FROM THE HUSTLE AND BUSTLE
AND SPEND SOME TIME IN CENTRAL PARK.
IT IS THE MOST VISITED PARK IN THE UNITED
STATES, BUT IT IS SO BIG THAT IT NEVER FEELS
TOO BUSY. LADY LIBERTY IS SO WELL LOVED
THAT SHE ENTERTAINS MANY VISITORS TOO.

Arlo takes a little break on a Central Park bench.
What a great place to rest and make new friends!

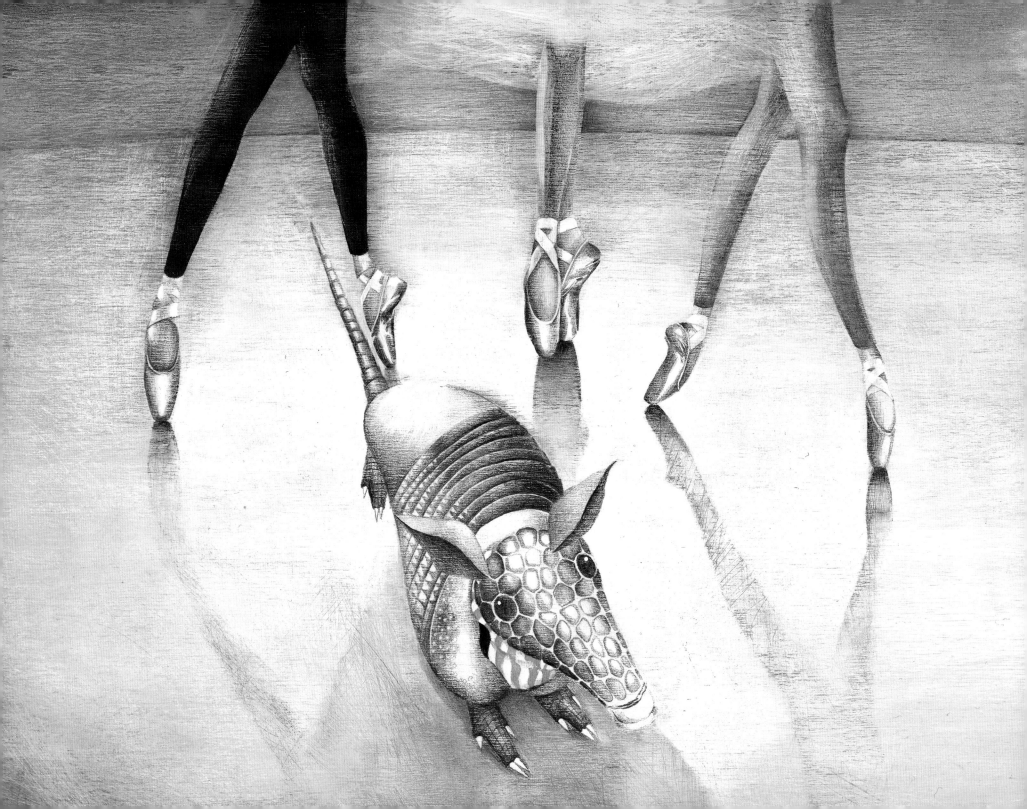

NEXT UP IS THE LINCOLN CENTER. HERE YOU CAN WATCH ALL SORTS OF DAZZLING PERFORMANCES: BALLET, OPERA, SYMPHONY AND THEATER. LADY LIBERTY'S FEET HAVE ALWAYS BEEN TOO LARGE FOR BALLET SHOES, BUT SHE HAS HAD A FEW OPERA CAMEOS.

Arlo tries an arabesque and a pirouette on stage with some ballet dancers. Dancing is tricky for an armadillo! Arlo thinks he might do better with Lady Liberty at the opera.

HEAD TO YANKEE STADIUM TO WATCH A NEW YORK YANKEES BASEBALL GAME. THIS TEAM IS LEGENDARY, AND MANY OF ITS PLAYERS CAN BE FOUND IN THE NATIONAL BASEBALL HALL OF FAME. LADY LIBERTY IS OFTEN SPOTTED AT THE GAMES BUT LIKES TO KEEP A LOW PROFILE.

Arlo gets a box of Cracker Jack and settles in for an afternoon of home runs, strikeouts and fly balls. He keeps an eye out for Lady Liberty in the crowd. Where could she be?

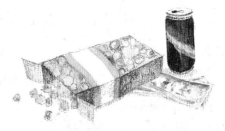

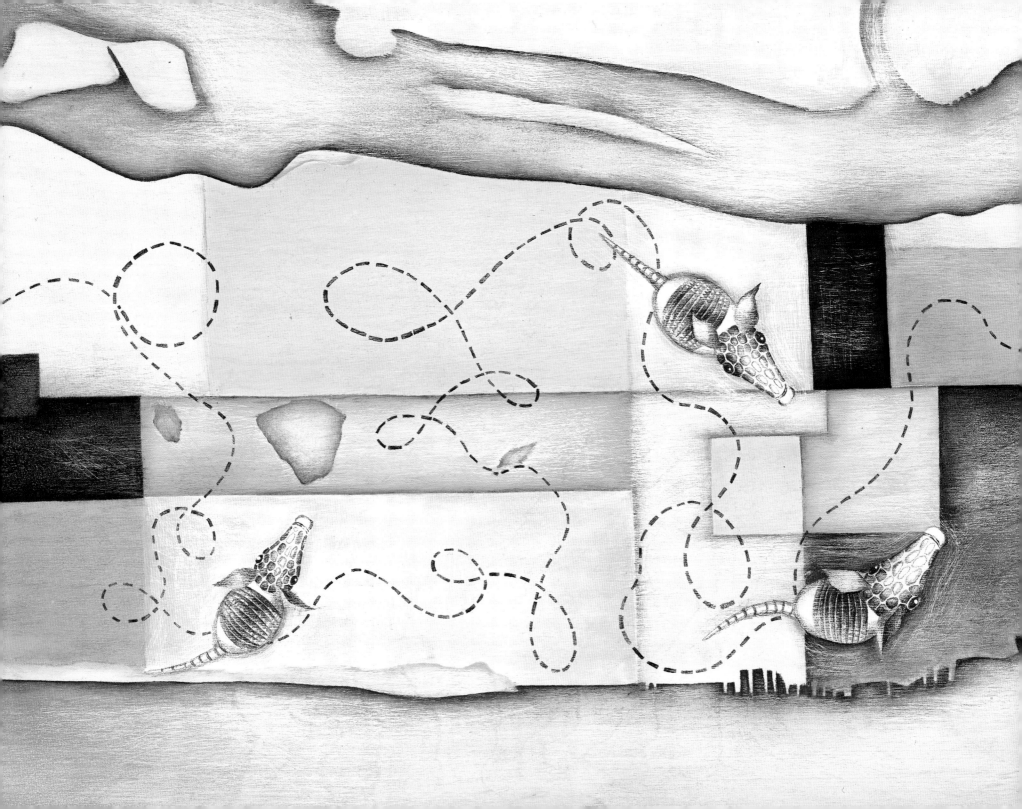

WANDER AROUND ALL THE
DIFFERENT NEIGHBORHOODS,
AND YOU WILL SEE CULTURES
FROM ALL OVER THE WORLD
— PEOPLE WHO HAVE COME TO
MAKE NEW YORK THEIR HOME
JUST LIKE LADY LIBERTY.

Arlo strolls around the neighborhoods, taking in the sights,
sounds and smells of many different countries. He picks up
some gifts for Lady Liberty from all the places he visits.

ARLO, YOU MUST WALK OVER THE BROOKLYN BRIDGE. WHEN IT WAS FIRST BUILT, IT WAS SO ADVANCED THAT CIRCUS MASTER P.T. BARNUM PARADED 21 ELEPHANTS ACROSS THE BRIDGE TO PROVE IT WAS SAFE. LADY LIBERTY WAS QUITE A MARVEL TOO, SPORTING A CUTTING-EDGE COPPER OUTFIT.

Arlo walks across the Brooklyn Bridge and imagines a parade of elephants crossing with him. Lady Liberty's copper outfit must be quite heavy; could it weigh as much as 21 elephants?

You are almost there, Arlo. Hop on the ferry at Battery Park and make your way to Liberty Island. Step off the boat and look up!

Arlo looks out over the ferry railing, watching the boats in the harbor. What a grand view Lady Liberty must have of the New York skyline!

Lady Liberty is the Statue of Liberty! Arlo looks up at her in wonder, dazzled by her towering height and beautiful aqua dress. She is the most striking statue he has ever seen. Just like Augustin, Arlo knows that this is the first of many visits with Lady Liberty . . . and with New York City.

TA-DA!
LADY LIBERTY!

ALL ABOUT LADY LIBERTY

The Statue of Liberty is about 46 meters or 151 feet tall.

Lady Liberty stands on Liberty Island in New York Harbor, 2.5 kilometers or 1.58 miles away from the bright city lights of New York City.

The Statue of Liberty is holding a tablet in her left hand inscribed with the date of the Declaration of Independence: July 4, 1776.

Lady Liberty functioned as a lighthouse from 1886 to 1902. Her gold torch is covered in 24-karat gold sheets and can be seen almost 39 kilometers or 24 miles out at sea!

The statue was a gift from France to the United States and was created by sculptor Frédéric Bartholdi and structural engineer Gustave Eiffel.

Approximately 4 million visitors visit the Statue of Liberty every year. That's a lot of new friends!

Lady Liberty's feet are 7.6 meters or 25 feet long. That means her shoe size is 879!

Lady Liberty can be spotted everywhere — on coffee mugs, New York license plates and even the US 10-dollar bill!

New York City is filled with people from all over the world. In the past, the statue was the first glimpse immigrants had of their new home.

Liberty

The Statue of Liberty has an iron frame and is covered in copper the same thickness as two pennies. She weighs 204,116 kilograms or 450,000 pounds. That's the same as 81 million pennies!

IAN - - 2023
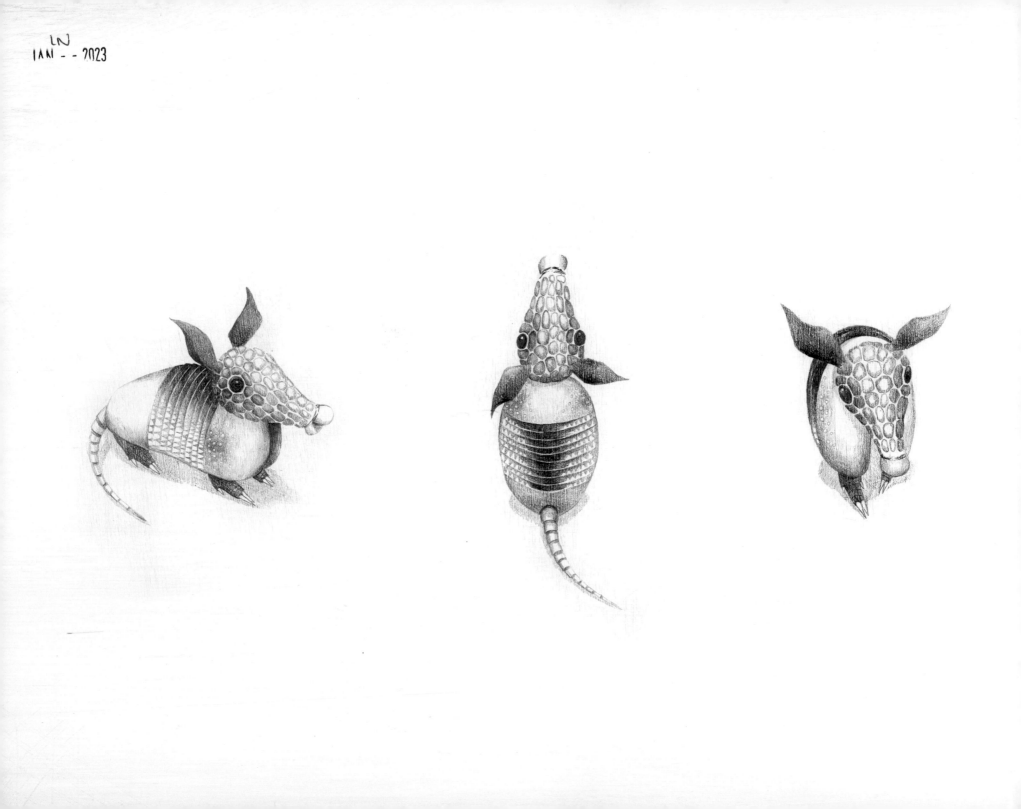